STEPHANIE PHILLIPS ★ GIULIA LALLI

EIGHT LIMBS

Life Drawn by Humanoids

STEPHANIE PHILLIPS
WRITER

GIULIA LALLI
ARTIST

LEE LOUGHRIDGE
COLORIST

ANDWORLD DESIGN'S JAME
LETTERER

DAN PANOSIAN
COVER ARTIST

KHOI PHAM & LEE LOUGHRIDGE
TITLE PAGE ILLUSTRATION

JAKE THOMAS & ROB LEVIN EDITORS **SANDY TANAKA** SENIOR DESIGNER
JERRY FRISSEN SENIOR ART DIRECTOR **FABRICE GIGER** PUBLISHER

Rights and Licensing - licensing@humanoids.com
Press and Social Media - pr@humanoids.com

Library of Congress Control Number: 2023933893

Life Drawn is an imprint of Humanoids, Inc.

WHY WE FIGHT

INTRODUCTION BY STEPHANIE PHILLIPS
WITH UFC FIGHTER JESSICA-ROSE "JESSY JESS" CLARK

"Why would you want to ruin your pretty face?"

I was asked this question, or iterations of it, repeatedly during the years I spent fighting and coaching Muay Thai. Stepping into the ring is inherently dangerous—Muay Thai fighters can use elbows, knees, shins, and fists against our opponents to inflict as much damage as possible and win a fight, and that comes with some pretty obvious consequences. I'm no stranger to bloody noses, bruises, welts, broken bones, and cuts from my time fighting. But I also couldn't help but notice that, for men, those cuts and bruises are worn like a badge of honor while the bloodied female face is seen as unattractive and even reminiscent of **victimization**.

Nothing could be further from the truth.

The blood, cuts, bruises, welts...they are symbols of commitment and the effort that we give to this sport. Our bodies are constantly placed under scrutiny, but the choice to participate in Muay Thai and other Martial Arts allowed me to turn my own body into a site of resistance against the norms that are typically placed on female bodies. The blood represents my choice—my choice to train and build strength, and my ***choice*** to step into the ring.

The bloodied face of a female fighter is beautiful.

It is strength.

And Muay Thai hasn't just been my own personal road to self-discovery, but has led to many women finding themselves inside a ring or an octagon, with padded gloves strapped to their fists. Jessica-Rose Clark, a professional fighter currently competing in the women's Bantamweight division of the Ultimate Fighting Championship (UFC), got an early look at EIGHT LIMBS and wrote:

> "For me, in my life, martial arts and combat sports have been the one thing that has allowed me to figure out who I truly am at my core. There is nothing like the feeling of being locked in a cage, or crossing over the ropes of the ring, knowing that in that moment the only things you can rely on are your heart and the level of effort you gave in preparation. Everything is laid bare. Your soul and who you are at your core, are on display for everyone to see. It is the greatest feeling in the world."
>
> —Jessica-Rose Clark, February 2023

I wrote EIGHT LIMBS as a celebration of what it means to ***choose*** to fight. As the story discusses, there is a vast difference between fighting and violence, and I think that boils down to ***choice***. There is strength in the choice we make to learn to fight and train our bodies to participate in one of the most difficult and dangerous sports in the world. That's not to say Muay Thai is the only way for women to resist gendered norms...but it was mine and it means the world to me. Muay Thai is more than a sport to me, and learning to fight taught me to respect and love myself in a way I never did before.

—Stephanie Phillips, February 2023

CHAPTER 1

KRAK
FIGHT!
FIVE DOLLARS SAYS MARI KICKS HER ASS!
YOU BITCH!
GET HER!
HEY!
GET OFF OF HER!
UNGH!
THAT'S ENOUGH!
"I WOULD CERTAINLY UNDERSTAND IF THIS WERE AN ISOLATED INCIDENT..."

"...BUT THIS IS THE THIRD INFRACTION THIS MONTH ALONE..."
...SKIPPING SCHOOL, DISRESPECTING TEACHERS AND PEERS, AND NOW FIGHTING...
WE ARE WORKING TO ADDRESS ALL OF THESE ISSUES, OF COURSE. MARI'S SITUATION IS JUST... UNIQUE.
WHILE I CERTAINLY WISH TO SUPPORT ALL OF OUR STUDENTS, AND I UNDERSTAND YOUR POSITION AS MARI'S CASEWORKER...
...I NO LONGER THINK WE CAN OFFER MARI WHAT SHE NEEDS TO SUCCEED WHILE ALSO LOOKING OUT FOR THE REST OF THE STUDENT BODY HERE AT ELMWOOD.
YOU'RE KICKING HER OUT?
I AM SORRY, BUT I HAVE TO THINK OF THE OTHER STUDENTS. MARI HAS BEEN GIVEN A NUMBER OF WARNINGS ABOUT THESE ISSUES...
AND, AT THIS POINT, IT MIGHT BE THE ONLY WAY TO APPEASE JULIA'S PARENTS, WHO ARE THREATENING TO PRESS CHARGES.
THIS IS THE SECOND SCHOOL THIS YEAR.

LOOK, I AM NOT UNSYMPATHETIC TO THE CIRCUMSTANCES.
IF YOU'D LIKE, I COULD MAKE A CALL TO ROGER'S PREPARATORY SCHOOL. THEY ARE FAR BETTER EQUIPPED TO DEAL WITH... WITH THESE KINDS OF ISSUES.
WITHOUT A SCHOLARSHIP...
... I JUST DON'T KNOW HOW WE COULD MAKE THAT WORK.
ESPECIALLY SINCE WE'RE STILL LOOKING FOR A NEW FOSTER HOME.
I UNDERSTAND IT'S A DIFFICULT SITUATION...
...LIKE I SAID, WE'D BE HAPPY TO HELP MARI TRANSITION TO A NEW INSTITUTION...
...BUT WE ARE NO LONGER ABLE TO ACCOMMODATE HER HERE AT ELMWOOD.
"YOUR FIST IS AN EXTENSION OF YOUR ENTIRE BODY..."

...THE GOAL IS TO MAINTAIN CONTROL OF EVERY MUSCLE...
...KEEP UPRIGHT AND BALANCED...
....AND ALLOW EACH MOVEMENT TO FLOW INTO THE NEXT...
...USING YOUR WEIGHT DISTRIBUTION TO GENERATE POWER.
THIS IS ABOUT FLOW. NOT STRENGTH.
PRACTICE IMAGINING YOUR OPPONENT. IMAGINE YOUR REACTIONS TO WHAT THEY MIGHT THROW AT YOU.
THEY THROW. YOU ***RESPOND.***
LIKE PUZZLE PIECES.

REMEMBER, WE NEED TO WORK ON KEEPING BALANCE NO MATTER WHAT MOVE WE'RE THROWING.
VERY GOOD...
...KEEP YOUR CHIN TUCKED.
BEEP
BEEP
BEEP

ALL RIGHT... GREAT CLASS EVERYONE!
GREAT WORK.
DON'T FORGET, TUESDAY AT FIVE WE WILL HAVE AN OPEN MAT AND TECHNIQUE IS MOVED TO SIX.
THANKS, COACH JOANNA.
LITTLE VICTORIA WANTED TO SAY HELLO TO EVERYONE!
SHE'S SO CUTE! AND I BET SHE'LL BE A FIGHTER JUST LIKE YOU TWO.
OUR NEXT STRAW WEIGHT CHAMPION.
RUNS IN THE FAMILY.

FREESTYLE MUAY THAI
HAVE A GOOD NIGHT!
YOU READY...?
...OR DO YOU WANT TO WARM UP FIRST?
I'VE BEEN IN THE GYM ALL NIGHT. I'M GOOD.
YOU GOT THIRTY MINUTES IN YOU?
KNEE'S BEEN BAD, BUT I THINK I CAN DO IT.
A KID IN THE BEGINNERS' CLASS MISSED THE PAD EARLIER AND NEARLY TOOK ME OUT...
...I TOLD THEM TO EASE UP TO PRACTICE ON TECHNIQUE...
...BUT YOU KNOW HOW KIDS GET...

"...ALWAYS SOMETHING TO PROVE."
AND NOW... YOUR NEW STRAWWEIGHT CHAMPION OF THE WORLD...
CHAMPION
...JOANNA CARR!
YES!
"JOANNA...?"

CHAMPION
EARTH TO JOANNA...
...YOU OKAY, BABE?
YEAH... YEAH. JUST KIND OF SPACED OUT, I GUESS. IT'S BEEN A LONG DAY.
YOU SURE? CAUSE WE DON'T HAVE TO--
I'M GOOD. REALLY. LET'S GO.
TAKE IT SLOW.
...OR DON'T.
LIKE I SAID... IT'S BEEN A LONG DAY.

WHACK
"...AND CARR TAKES A STRONG SHOT TO THE HEAD...
"OH! AND CARR WITH THE RETURN THAT DOESN'T LAND!
"CARR JUST CAN'T SEEM TO FIND HER RHYTHM TONIGHT, FOLKS!
BREATHE, JO.

WHACK
"ANDRE THROWS... AND CARR JUST BARELY DODGES THAT ONE...
"AND ANDRE FINDS HER SWEET SPOT, TAGGING CARR WITH A RIGHT HOOK!"
HUH..?

...ARGH...
WHAT WOULD YOU TELL YOUR STUDENTS?
TO NOT BE A SMART ASS.
BALANCE.
I'M SLOW. I'VE BEEN SLOW SINCE VICTORIA... IF WE WERE FIGHTING, YOU WOULD HAVE TAGGED ME.
A LOT.
AND I FEEL LIKE MY LEFT HIP IS LOCKING OR SOMETHING WHEN I GO TO KICK... I'M DEFINITELY NOT FULLY ROTATING AND--
HEY... BREATHE.
WHEN I SAID BALANCE, I WASN'T JUST TALKING ABOUT YOU TRYING TO KICK THE SHIT OUT OF YOUR VERY LOVING, VERY SUPPORTIVE, AND VERY HANDSOME HUSBAND.
GIVE YOURSELF A BREAK. YOU'VE BEEN IN THE GYM ALL DAY.
AND IT'S NOT LIKE YOU'RE ABOUT TO STEP INTO THE RING AGAIN ANYTIME SOON...
MAYBE RETIRING WAS A MISTAKE.

WHAT'S THAT, VICTORIA?
YOU THINK MOMMY SHOULD HAVE RETIRED THE FIRST TIME SHE HAD KNEE SURGERY BEFORE THE AGE OF THIRTY?
YOU'RE INSUFFERABLE.
DON'T SHOOT THE MESSENGER.
THAT WAS THE BABY TALKING... NOT ME.
LOOK, I KNOW HOW BADLY YOU WANTED TO KEEP FIGHTING. I'VE ALWAYS BEEN IN YOUR CORNER... I ALWAYS WILL BE.
BUT WE BOTH KNEW THERE'D BE A LIMIT.
YEAH... I KNOW, I KNOW...
...IT'S WHAT'S BEST FOR ALL OF US.
WELL, I THINK WHAT'S BEST FOR ALL OF US...

"...ARE TACOS AND QUESO FROM RUBIOS."
NO, YOU DO NOT GET TO BACK OUT NOW, CLARK! YOU MADE THE BET!
UH-UH... I THINK YOU SHOULD BE PAYING ME FOR LETTING ME MARRY YOU UNDER FALSE PRETENSES.
HAD I KNOWN YOU KNEW ALL OF THE LYRICS TO THAT NUMA-NUMA SONG--
JOANNA...!
ELLIE?
WHAT ARE YOU DOING HERE...?
IS EVERYTHING OKAY?
JOANNA... CLARK... I'M SO SORRY TO SHOW UP UNANNOUNCED LIKE THIS.

NOT AT ALL... YOU'RE ALWAYS WELCOME.
BUT DRIVING THREE HOURS INSTEAD OF JUST CALLING--
I... I THOUGHT I'D TALK TO YOU IN PERSON. I DIDN'T WANT TO ASK...
...BUT I... NEED A *FAVOR*...
COME, LET'S TALK INSIDE.
WE'LL MAKE COFFEE.
"HER NAME IS *MARI*..."

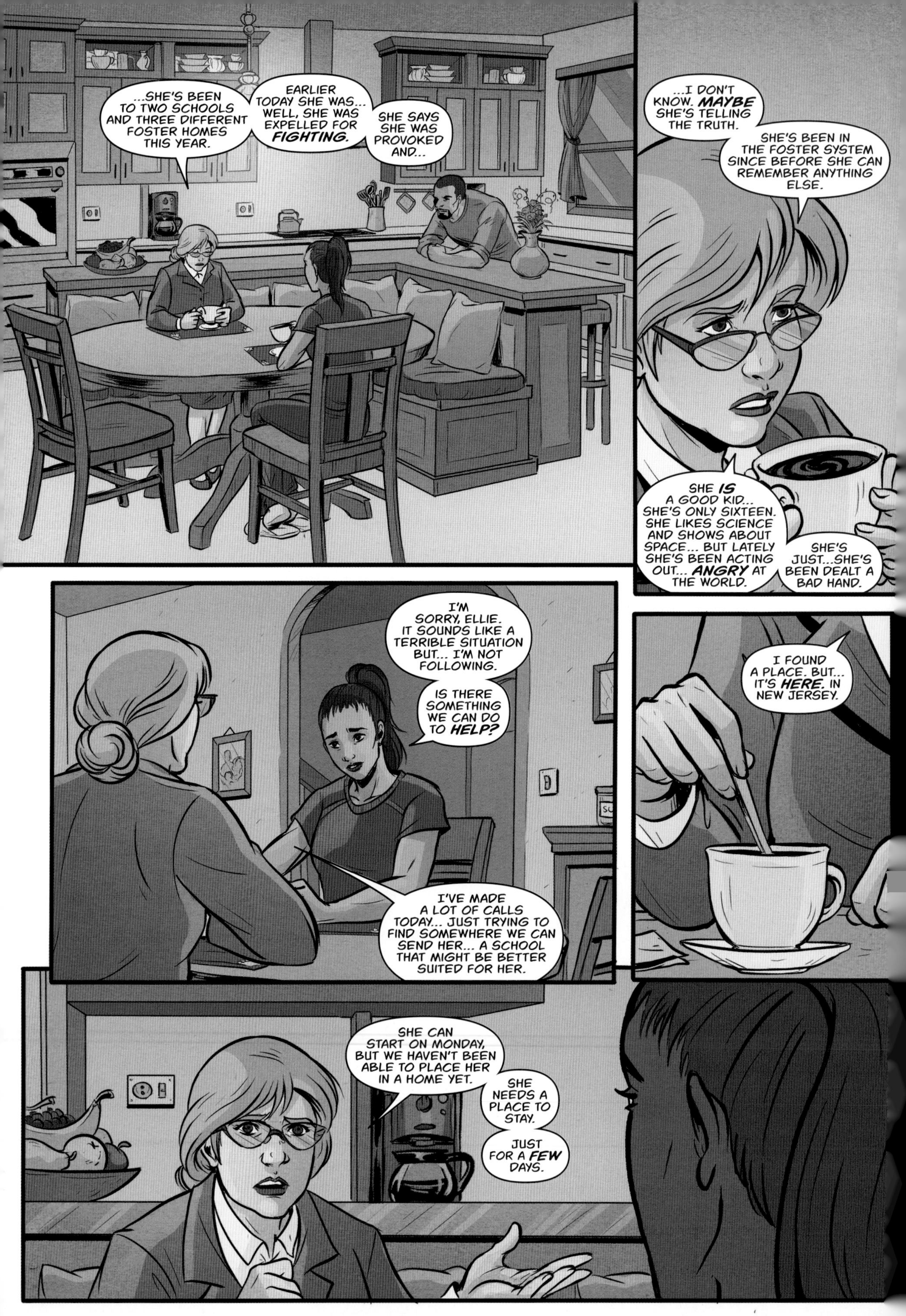

...SHE'S BEEN TO TWO SCHOOLS AND THREE DIFFERENT FOSTER HOMES THIS YEAR.
EARLIER TODAY SHE WAS... WELL, SHE WAS EXPELLED FOR FIGHTING.
SHE SAYS SHE WAS PROVOKED AND...
...I DON'T KNOW. MAYBE SHE'S TELLING THE TRUTH.
SHE'S BEEN IN THE FOSTER SYSTEM SINCE BEFORE SHE CAN REMEMBER ANYTHING ELSE.
SHE IS A GOOD KID... SHE'S ONLY SIXTEEN. SHE LIKES SCIENCE AND SHOWS ABOUT SPACE... BUT LATELY SHE'S BEEN ACTING OUT... ANGRY AT THE WORLD.
SHE'S JUST...SHE'S BEEN DEALT A BAD HAND.
I'M SORRY, ELLIE. IT SOUNDS LIKE A TERRIBLE SITUATION BUT... I'M NOT FOLLOWING.
IS THERE SOMETHING WE CAN DO TO HELP?
I'VE MADE A LOT OF CALLS TODAY... JUST TRYING TO FIND SOMEWHERE WE CAN SEND HER... A SCHOOL THAT MIGHT BE BETTER SUITED FOR HER.
I FOUND A PLACE. BUT... IT'S HERE. IN NEW JERSEY.
SHE CAN START ON MONDAY, BUT WE HAVEN'T BEEN ABLE TO PLACE HER IN A HOME YET.
SHE NEEDS A PLACE TO STAY.
JUST FOR A FEW DAYS.

WELL, I THINK WE WOULD NEED TO TALK ABOUT IT...
SHE CAN STAY HERE.
REALLY?
FOR A FEW DAYS.
THIS IS... THIS IS SO GREAT. YOU HAVE NO IDEA WHAT A RELIEF--

I'LL NEED TO MAKE SOME CALLS, GET THE ARRANGEMENTS IN ORDER...
WELL, IT'S A GOOD THING WE'RE ON THE SAME PAGE ABOUT ACCEPTING A STRANGE TEENAGER INTO OUR HOME OR ELSE THIS WOULD BE A LITTLE AWKWARD.
AND WHAT DID YOU WANT ME TO SAY? THE KID NEEDS HELP AND IT'S ONLY FOR A LITTLE BIT.
I'VE KNOWN ELLIE FOR TWENTY YEARS... YOU KNOW HOW MANY TIMES SHE'S HELPED ME OUT?
DON'T YOU THINK WE SHOULD AT LEAST CONSIDER THE SITUATION FOR VICTORIA? WE HAVE A BABY, JO.
ELLIE SAID IT HERSELF... THIS KID ISN'T EXACTLY A MODEL CITIZEN.
BECAUSE YOU AND I BOTH HAD SUCH PRISTINE CHILDHOODS...
IT'S ONLY A FEW DAYS, AND MAYBE A LITTLE KINDNESS COULD DO HER SOME GOOD. BESIDES...

"...I'M PRETTY SURE I KNOW HOW TO HANDLE A TEENAGED GIRL."
WHAT DO YOU THINK...?
WILL THIS WORK FOR YOU, MARI?
SURE.
OH, WE GOT YOU A LITTLE SOMETHING... JUST A WELCOME PRESENT.

KRSH
THEY'RE BOXING GLOVES. I THINK ELLIE TOLD YOU THAT WE OWN A GYM SO I THOUGHT...
...MAYBE ONE DAY AFTER SCHOOL YOU'D LIKE TO GIVE IT A TRY AND JOIN IN ON A CLASS.
I MEAN... ONLY IF YOU WANT, OF COURSE. THERE'S NO PRESSURE.
YOU COULD EVEN TRY THEM ON AND SEE IF THEY FIT, OR--
NOT NOW.
I'M JUST GOING TO GO TO SLEEP.
YEAH, SURE. I BET YOU'VE HAD A LONG DAY.
SLEEP WELL AND LET US KNOW IF THERE'S ANYTHING ELSE YOU NEED.
"THAT'S NOT WHAT A LITTLE GIRL NEEDS..."

...NO GIRL NEEDS BOXING GLOVES...
...WHAT WERE YOU THINKING?
I THOUGHT SHE'D HAVE A LITTLE FUN. WHAT THE HELL'S SO WRONG WITH THAT?
SHE'S MY DAUGHTER, TOO!
HOW GODDAMN CONVENIENT... YOU SHOW UP WHENEVER YOU WANT AND PLAY THE HERO.
WHAT D'YA WANT ME TO DO, HUH? MAKE THE KID LIKE ME LESS?
I JUST HOPE YOU'RE HERE WHEN SHE GETS HURT WITH THOSE THINGS BECAUSE I'M NOT DEALING WITH IT.
YOU'RE NOT GONNA GET HURT, ARE YA, JOANNA?
OF COURSE NOT... 'CAUSE I'M GONNA TO TEACH YOU HOW TO THROW A PROPER PUNCH.
"SHE DIDN'T LIKE THE GLOVES..."

...SHE PRACTICALLY THREW THEM TO THE SIDE.
SHE JUST GOT THROWN INTO THE HOUSE OF COMPLETE STRANGERS. GIVE HER A LITTLE TIME TO ADJUST.
SHIT... SHE BIT ME.
DAMNIT. I DON'T KNOW WHY SHE WON'T LATCH...
WAGH!
SHHH... IT'S OKAY, MOMMY'S GOT YOU.
SHE NEEDS TO EAT. I DON'T KNOW WHAT I'M DOING WRONG.
YOU'RE NOT DOING ANYTHING WRONG.
DON'T YOU REMEMBER WHAT THE DOCTOR SAID...?
THERE'S NO SHAME IN GIVING HER A BOTTLE.

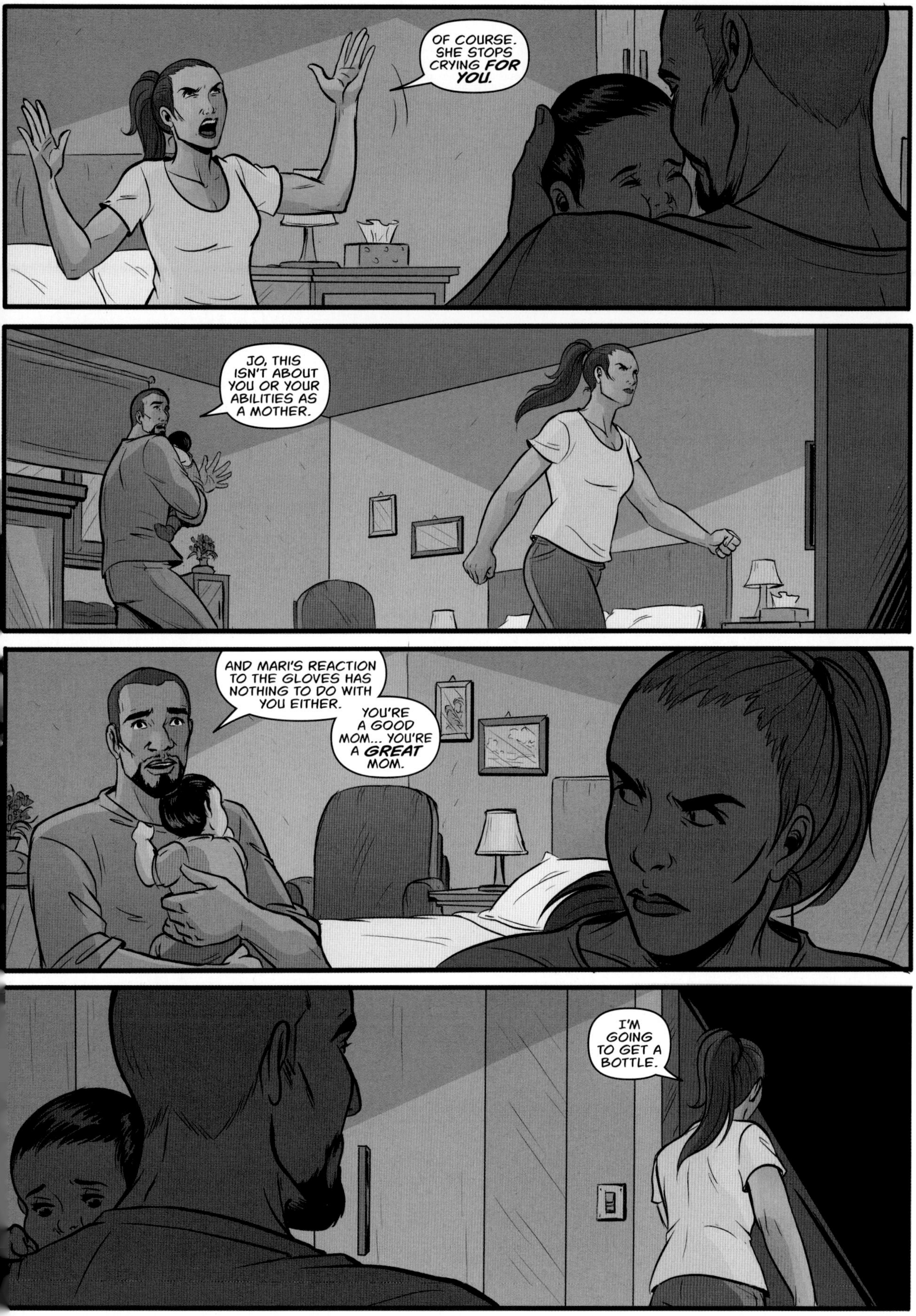
OF COURSE. SHE STOPS CRYING *FOR YOU.*
JO, THIS ISN'T ABOUT YOU OR YOUR ABILITIES AS A MOTHER.
AND MARI'S REACTION TO THE GLOVES HAS NOTHING TO DO WITH YOU EITHER.
YOU'RE A GOOD MOM... YOU'RE A *GREAT* MOM.
I'M GOING TO GET A BOTTLE.

FREESTYLE MUAY THAI
TODAY WE'RE WORKING ON TECHNICAL SPARRING...
...THE GOAL IS NOT TO HURT YOUR PARTNER...
...BUT FOCUS ON TECHNIQUE AND CONTROL.
GOOD REACTIONS, SARAH.
IF YOU BLOCK HIS KICK, RESPOND IMMEDIATELY. DON'T GIVE HIM TIME TO THINK OR RESET.

WHAK
THWAK
YOU KNOW, YOU'RE WELCOME TO USE THE EQUIPMENT...
THERE'S PLENTY OF SPACE IF YOU WANT TO USE THE JUMP ROPES OR TRY OUT YOUR NEW GLOVES ON THE BAGS.
I'M GOOD.
WHAT TIME ARE WE LEAVING?
CLARK WILL BE HERE AT FIVE TO PICK YOU UP.

I DON'T THINK ELLIE WOULD LIKE ME SAYING THIS, BUT IF YOU'RE GOING TO FIGHT, YOU SHOULD LEARN HOW TO DO IT RIGHT.
I KNOW HOW TO FIGHT.
THAT BRUISE? MEANS YOU TUCKED YOUR THUMB.
DO THAT WHEN YOU PUNCH AND YOU'LL HURT YOURSELF WAY MORE THAN THE OTHER GUY.
I'D BE HAPPY TO SHOW YOU HOW TO DO IT RIGHT...

...BUT IF YOU THINK YOU ALREADY KNOW HOW TO PUNCH, THAT'S COOL.
ALL RIGHT... ***BAG BURNOUTS!***
ONE-HUNDRED RIGHT...
ONE-HUNDRED LEFT.
REPEAT WITH TEEPS AND KNEES.
YOU KNOW THE DRILL.

GO!
PRETTY COOL, HUH?
SHE'D LET YOU JOIN IF YOU WANTED.
IT'S *KICKBOXING?*
NO, IT'S *MUAY THAI.*
WHAT'S THE DIFFERENCE?

OH, MUAY THAI IS WAY MORE DANGEROUS. WE GET TO USE KNEES, ELBOWS, CLINCH... BASICALLY ALL KINDS OF WAYS TO HURT YOUR OPPONENT.
YOU FIGHT, TOO?
I DID... BUT I WAS NOWHERE NEAR AS GOOD AS JOANNA.
YOU KNOW SHE'S A WORLD CHAMPION?
WHAT?
OH YEAH. CHECK THAT OUT. THEY DON'T GIVE A SERIOUS PIECE OF HARDWARE LIKE THAT TO JUST ANYONE.
JOANNA'S THE REAL DEAL. SHE WAS THE BEST FIGHTER I EVER WORKED WITH.
BUT SHE DOESN'T FIGHT ANYMORE?
WELL, I DID SAY THIS SPORT IS DANGEROUS, DIDN'T I?
WE CAN ALL ONLY FIGHT SO LONG BEFORE OUR BODIES CAN'T TAKE IT.
WE'RE NOT YOUNG LIKE YOU ANYMORE.
MY BACK IS HURTING JUST SITTING LIKE THIS.
YOU READY TO HEAD OUT? WE CAN PICK UP DINNER ON THE WAY BACK.

THERE'S A REALLY GREAT PIZZA PLACE RIGHT BY VICTORIA'S DAYCARE IF THAT SOUNDS GOOD TO YOU.
YEAH, THAT'S... COOL.
I'M A PEPPERONI GUY, BUT WE COULD DO HALF AND HALF IF YOU'D PREFER SOMETHING ELSE.
THEY'VE GOT A MEAN MEAT LOVER'S, TOO.

CHAPTER 2

SHE'S BEING MORE ACTIVE. YOU'RE NOT SCORING POINTS BY JUST BLOCKING.
YOU NEED TO REACT, JOANNA.
LOOK FOR ANGLES... SHE'S BEING A BULLDOG... COMING AT YOU WITH JUST STRENGTH. SHE WANTS TO THROW YOU OFF YOUR GAME.
STAY IN CONTROL.
DING

"CARR AND ANDRE ARE BACK AT IT FOR ROUND TWO OF THIS STRAW WEIGHT BOUT...
KEEP IT CLEAN...
"BUT THE QUESTION ON EVERYONE'S MIND... WILL JOANNA CARR RETAIN HER TITLE...?"

"...OR WILL WE SEE THE BELT ON A NEWCOMER'S WAIST TONIGHT?
"AND IT'S ANDRE WITH THE FIRST SHOT OF THE ROUND...
"CARR TRIES TO RESPOND...
"BUT ANDRE HAS AN ANSWER!
"THERE'S POWER... BUT NO ACCURACY THERE, FOLKS.
"...AND ANDRE CATCHES THE KICK...
"SENDING THE FORMER CHAMP TO THE MAT!

"CARR JUST DOESN'T EVEN HAVE A CHANCE TO BREATHE HERE.
"CARR CHARGES ANDRE...
"...AND JUST THROWS WILD PUNCHES.
"WOW... FOLKS, I AM SHOCKED. WHAT A DOMINANT PERFORMANCE FROM ANDRE TONIGHT.
"I HAVE TO SAY..."

"...I DON'T THINK I'VE EVER SEEN JOANNA CARR STRUGGLE WITH A RESPONSE LIKE THIS."
I COULD HELP YOU WITH THAT...

...IF YOU WANT TO PUT THE OTHER ONE ON AND SEE HOW THEY FEEL.
IT'S KIND OF TOUGH TO GET THEM TIGHT ONCE THEY'RE ON YOUR HANDS.
AT LEAST THESE ARE THE ONES WITH VELCRO AND NOT TIES.
WITH THE VELCRO ONES I CAN USE MY TEETH TO TRY TO GET THEM TIGHT IF NO ONE IS AROUND TO HELP ME.
IT LOOKS SILLY, BUT IT WORKS.
STICK YOUR HAND IN THERE.
WE'LL GET YOU SOME WRAPS TO PROTECT YOUR KNUCKLES AND KEEP THE GLOVES ON TIGHTER, BUT I'D SAY THEY LOOK PRETTY GOOD.

I GET TO KEEP THESE?
THEY WOULDN'T BE MUCH OF A GIFT IF YOU DIDN'T GET TO KEEP THEM.
HOW DO THEY FEEL?
I THINK... I THINK THEY FEEL GOOD. I DON'T KNOW WHAT THEY'RE SUPPOSED TO FEEL LIKE.
CAN YOU MOVE WITH THEM?
YEAH, THAT LOOKS GOOD.

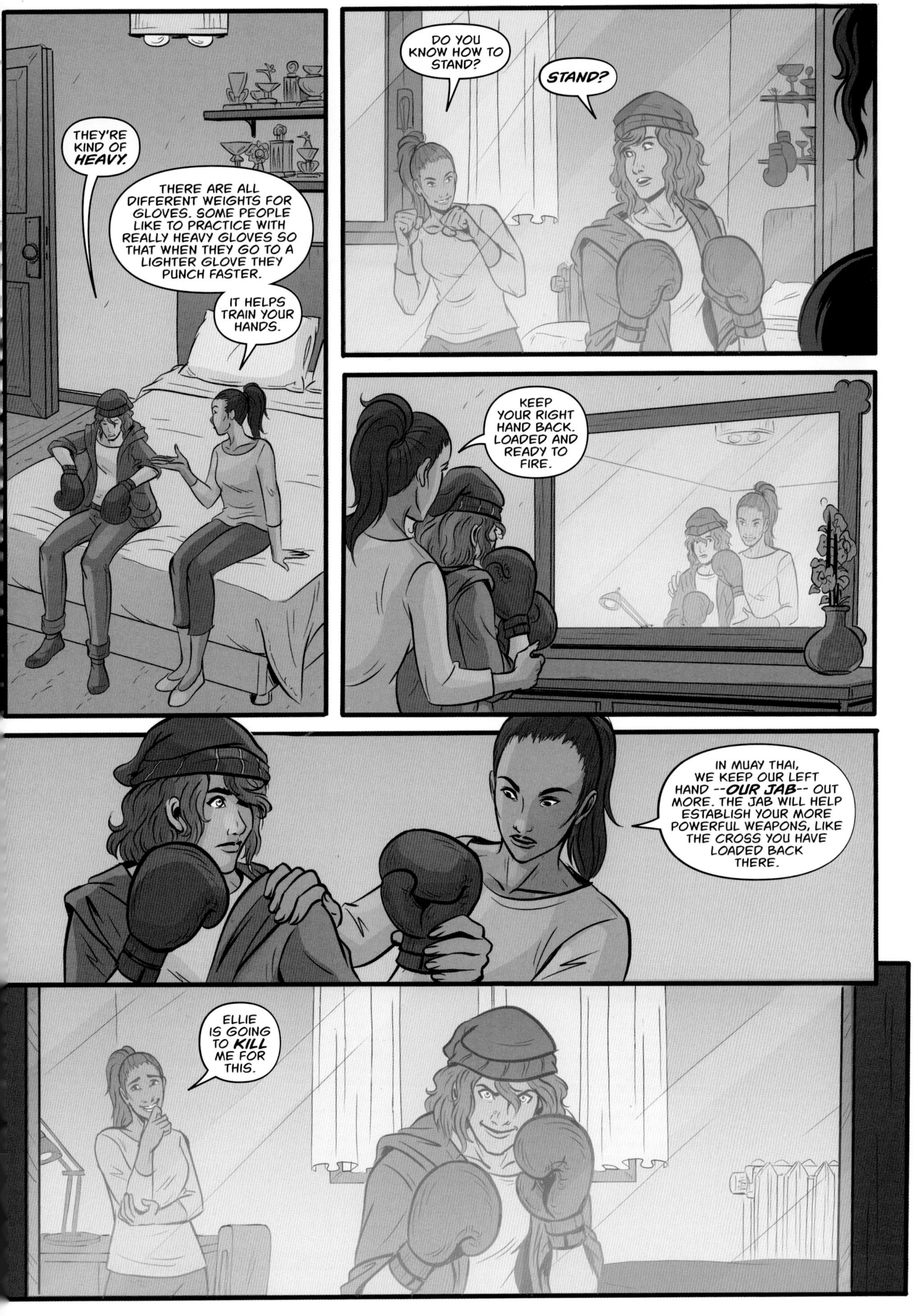
THEY'RE KIND OF **HEAVY.**
THERE ARE ALL DIFFERENT WEIGHTS FOR GLOVES. SOME PEOPLE LIKE TO PRACTICE WITH REALLY HEAVY GLOVES SO THAT WHEN THEY GO TO A LIGHTER GLOVE THEY PUNCH FASTER.
IT HELPS TRAIN YOUR HANDS.
DO YOU KNOW HOW TO STAND?
STAND?
KEEP YOUR RIGHT HAND BACK. LOADED AND READY TO FIRE.
IN MUAY THAI, WE KEEP OUR LEFT HAND --**OUR JAB**-- OUT MORE. THE JAB WILL HELP ESTABLISH YOUR MORE POWERFUL WEAPONS, LIKE THE CROSS YOU HAVE LOADED BACK THERE.
ELLIE IS GOING TO **KILL** ME FOR THIS.

DOES IT HURT?
DOES *WHAT* HURT?
GETTING PUNCHED. BEING IN A FIGHT. CLARK SAID YOU'VE HAD LOTS OF FIGHTS.
YEAH, I GUESS IT DOES. BUT YOU'RE NOT REALLY THINKING ABOUT THAT IN THE MOMENT.
I ONCE BROKE MY ANKLE IN THE FIRST ROUND OF A FIGHT AND DIDN'T NOTICE.
THAT'S *CRAZY.* HOW DID YOU NOT NOTICE A BROKEN ANKLE?
SOMETIMES WHEN ADRENALINE KICKS IN IT CAN HIDE THE PAIN.
BUT I WAS ALSO JUST FOCUSED ON THE FIGHT AND DIDN'T HAVE TIME TO DEAL WITH IT.
DID YOU *WIN?*
YUP. I FOUGHT TWO MORE ROUNDS AND THEN WENT TO THE E.R. WITH A MEDAL AROUND MY NECK.
THAT'S *SO* COOL.

SO, WHEN SOMEONE MAKES YOU MAD YOU COULD JUST--
I *COULD.* BUT THAT'S NOT THE POINT. MUAY THAI IS A SPORT AND IT'S ABOUT *CONTROL* AND *RESPECT.*
WHAT WE DO IN THE RING IS FIGHTING... PUNCHING SOMEONE ON THE STREET BECAUSE I'M MAD AT THEM IS *VIOLENCE.*
THAT'S THE SAME THING.
WELL, WHEN WE FIGHT... WE *CHOOSE* TO GET INTO THE RING.
WE *CHOOSE* TO PARTICIPATE IN A SPORT THAT *COULD* RESULT IN INJURY, BUT THE ULTIMATE GOAL IS SKILL.
I CAN TRY TO SHOW YOU WHAT I MEAN AT THE GYM TOMORROW.
AND I PROMISE IT'S MORE FUN WHEN YOU ACTUALLY GET TO PUNCH SOMETHING.

GREAT POWER...

...NOW WE NEED TO WORK ON CONTROL.

INSTEAD OF STANDING FLAT-FOOTED, SPACE YOUR LEGS OUT A BIT LIKE MINE.
THIS WILL HELP YOU KEEP YOUR BALANCE AND GENERATE POWER FROM THE TORQUE OF YOUR BACK LEG.
A LITTLE LIKE BASEBALL PLAYERS WHEN THEY SWING A BAT. THERE'S MORE POWER WHEN YOU ENGAGE YOUR HIPS AND NOT JUST YOUR ARMS.

NOW, LET YOUR HIP AND SHOULDER THROW YOUR FIST.
WHAK
PERFECT!
I KNEW YOU'D BE A NATURAL.
WE'RE GOING TO START CLASS IN A MOMENT, BUT THERE'S SOMETHING I'D LIKE YOU TO SEE FIRST.
YOU ASKED ABOUT THE DIFFERENCE BETWEEN WHAT WE DO AND VIOLENCE...

...SO TODAY WE'RE GOING TO START WITH A **WAI KRU** DEMONSTRATION.
I'M GOING TO MESS THIS UP.
WHEN YOU DO IT IN THE RING, WE WANT THIS TO BE MUSCLE MEMORY...

THAT'S WHY WE PRACTICE IT.

"THE WAI KRU IS BROKEN INTO TWO PARTS.
"FIRST, THE FIGHTER MOVES AROUND THE RING THREE TIMES TO SHOW RESPECT TO OUR COACHES, GYM, AND FAMILY.
"WE NEVER ACTUALLY ENTER THE RING ALONE AND THE WAI KRU GIVES THANKS TO THE SUPPORT THAT WE BRING TO EACH FIGHT.
"IT DEMONSTRATES TO THE AUDIENCE A FIGHTER'S POWER AND CONTROL...
"...AND SOMETIMES A BIT OF THEIR PERSONALITY BECAUSE FIGHTERS CAN CUSTOMIZE THE DANCE TO MAKE IT THEIR OWN.

"THE SECOND PORTION IS THE RAM MUAY... THE BOXING DANCE.
"IT'S A SERIES OF MOVEMENTS THAT LOOK A LITTLE LIKE DANCING.
"THE WAI KRU... THE RAM MUAY... BOTH ARE ABOUT RESPECT...
"...RESPECTING WHAT WE DO AND ACKNOWLEDGING THE TRADITIONS OF MUAY THAI."

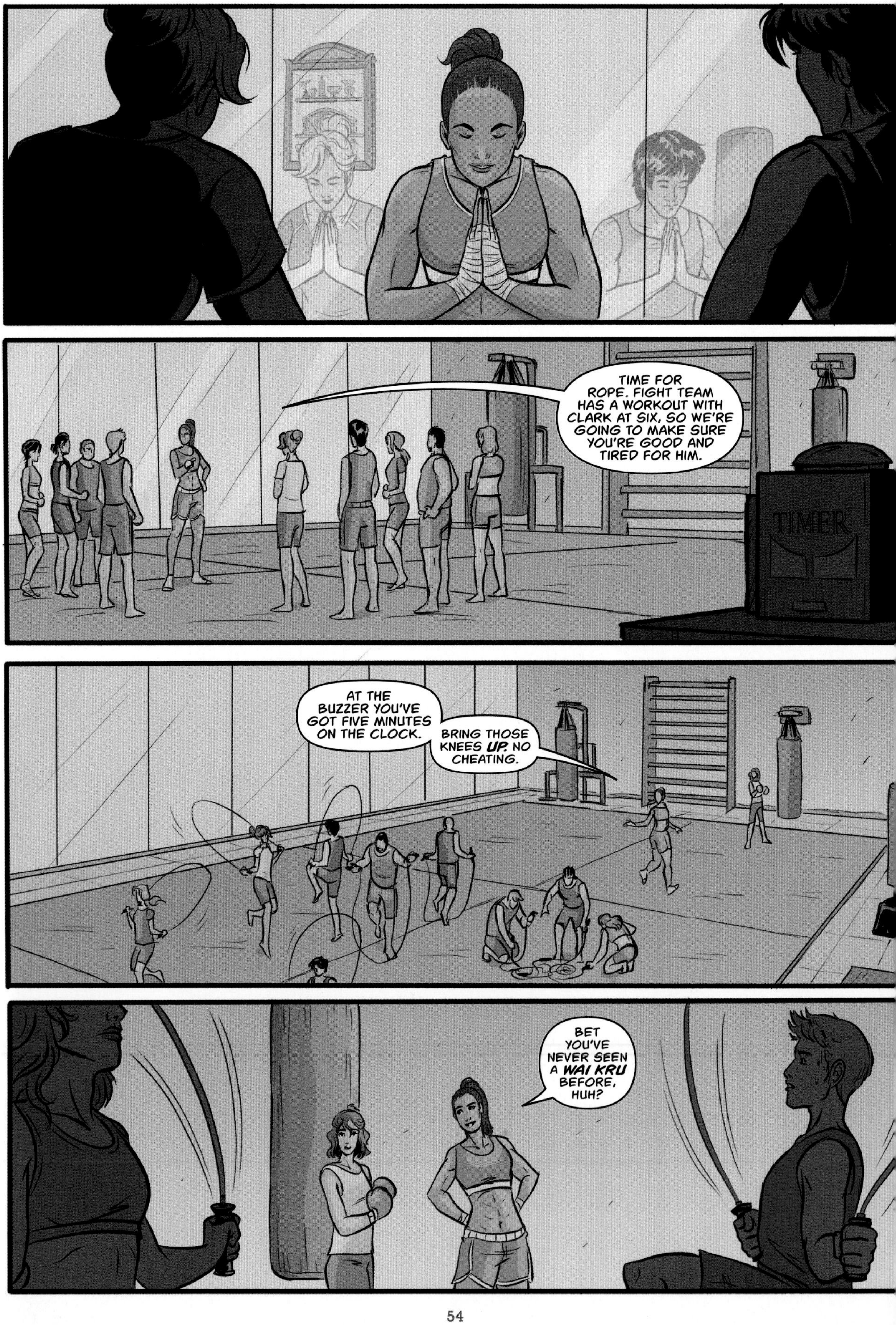
TIME FOR ROPE. FIGHT TEAM HAS A WORKOUT WITH CLARK AT SIX, SO WE'RE GOING TO MAKE SURE YOU'RE GOOD AND TIRED FOR HIM.
TIMER
AT THE BUZZER YOU'VE GOT FIVE MINUTES ON THE CLOCK.
BRING THOSE KNEES *UP.* NO CHEATING.
BET YOU'VE NEVER SEEN A ***WAI KRU*** BEFORE, HUH?

IT LOOKED... WEIRD.
IN THAI, WAI IS A SIGN OF RESPECT. THE DEEPER THE BOW AND THE HIGHER YOUR HANDS, THE MORE RESPECT YOU SHOW.
KRU MEANS TEACHERS, SO THE WAI KRU IS A RITUAL ABOUT RESPECT BETWEEN STUDENTS AND THEIR TEACHER.
AS A COACH AND TEACHER, MY RESPONSIBILITY IS TO ENCOURAGE MY STUDENTS AND WATCH THEIR GROWTH AS FIGHTERS.
SO, WE PERFORM THE WAI KRU AS A WAY TO SOLIDIFY THAT BOND -- TO SHOW RESPECT FOR EACH OTHER.
WE'RE FAMILY.
IT JUST LOOKED LIKE DANCING TO ME.

HOPEFULLY *PRETTY* DANCING.
BZZZZT
PARTNER UP!
GO CROSS FOR CROSS.
WE HAVE AN ODD NUMBER...
YOU'D BE DOING ME A HUGE FAVOR IF YOU'D JOIN THE CLASS TODAY, MARI.
I... I DON'T KNOW. I DON'T KNOW WHAT TO DO.
DON'T WORRY ABOUT IT... I'LL TELL YOU.
I PROMISE, YOU'LL PICK IT UP SUPER-FAST.

MARI, THIS IS JOYCE. YOU'LL BE PARTNERS FOR THIS FIRST DRILL.
WE'RE JUST WORKING ON THROWING A CROSS, BLOCKING THE CROSS, AND RETURNING WITH THE CROSS.
I THROW MY CROSS AND JOYCE BLOCKS OR DODGES...
...THEN I BLOCK.
YOU JUST KEEP IT GOING. THROW. BLOCK. THROW. BLOCK.
YOU THROW FIRST.

GOOD. YOU CAN GO A LITTLE HARDER THOUGH.
YOU WON'T HURT ME.
KEEP YOUR FACE COVERED WHILE I THROW.
GOOD. NOW WE CAN PICK UP THE PACE A LITTLE.
I'LL MATCH YOUR SPEED AND STRENGTH.
WHAK
OOF!

WHAT THE HELL!
I'M SO SORRY... I DIDN'T MEAN TO.
ARE YOU OKAY?
LEMME SEE...
NO... DON'T.
THIS IS SO STUPID.
IT'S NOT EVEN REAL FIGHTING.
MARI, WAIT...

MARI!
MARI?
MARI?!

KLING
OH, COME ON! HOW DO YOU MISS A FREE THROW?!

HEY...
...I SAW THAT!
DAVE
WE'RE CALLING THE POLICE, YOU LITTLE SHIT!
CALL THE POLICE, DARRYL. WE GOT A SHOPLIFTER...
NO... DON'T...
I'M SORRY... I DIDN'T MEAN--
MARI!

IS THIS YOUR CHILD?
SHE WAS STEALING AND WE'RE CALLING THE COPS.
DAVE
THEN YOU CAN EXPLAIN TO THE POLICE WHY YOU CALLED THEM ON A PERFECTLY INNOCENT GIRL WHO CAME HERE TO BUY CANDY.
I SAW HER PUT IT IN HER POCKET.
I'M NOT SEEING A SHOPPING CART ANYWHERE...
...AND WE NEED A LOT OF CANDY.
FINE. BUT YOU'RE BUYING ALL THE CANDY SHE SPILLED.
FINE. BUT WE'RE ALSO GETTING TWO SLURPEES.
DAVE

WHAT KIND DID YOU GET?
COKE.
BLUEBERRY'S BETTER.
WHY DID YOU HELP ME?
WHY WOULDN'T I? THOSE GUYS WERE BEING JERKS.
BUT I **WAS** STEALING.
I KNOW. WHAT HAPPENED?
YOU FORGOT ABOUT THE SECOND CLERK, DIDN'T YOU?
WHENEVER IT'S A BUSY TIME, LIKE RUSH HOUR, YOU ALWAYS HAVE TO KEEP AN EYE OUT FOR A SECOND EMPLOYEE.
WHY DO YOU KNOW THAT?
WHY... WHY AREN'T YOU **MAD?**
I **RUINED** YOUR CLASS AND RAN AWAY.
AND YOU... **BOUGHT CANDY.**

I USED TO COME HERE WHEN MY PARENTS ARGUED.
I HATE YELLING... THEY WOULD START AND IT WAS JUST LIKE THAT SENSATION YOU GET WHEN PEOPLE RUN THEIR NAILS ON A CHALKBOARD.
MY THING WAS TWIZZLERS. STEAL A PACK OF THOSE AND THEN SIT AT THE PARK UNTIL THE POLICE WOULD USUALLY FIND ME AND TAKE ME HOME.
WE HAD A WHOLE ROUTINE.
THEN, I GOT MY FIRST PAIR OF BOXING GLOVES. MY DAD KNEW SOME GUYS HE THOUGHT COULD TEACH ME.
I THINK HE WAS GAMBLING ON FIGHTS...
BUT DOESN'T MEAN I LOVED THE SPORT ANY LESS.
KARATE, BOXING, MUAY THAI...
I LOVED THEM ALL. THEY HELPED ME FOCUS. HELPED ME MAKE FRIENDS.
IT'S HOW I MET CLARK.
AND, I OWE YOU AN APOLOGY.
ME?

I PUSHED YOU. YOU REMIND ME A LOT OF **ME.**
AND SINCE MUAY THAI MEANS SO MUCH TO ME... I JUST THOUGHT MAYBE IT WOULD TO YOU, TOO.
BUT THAT WAS WRONG. **YOU** GET TO CHOOSE WHAT YOU LIKE AND DON'T.
I **DO** LIKE IT... BUT I'M NOT VERY GOOD.
NO ONE GETS GOOD AFTER A FIVE MINUTE LESSON.
THAT'S WHAT MAKES IT **FUN.** YOU GET TO LEARN AND GET BETTER.
THEN YOU CAN KICK EVERYONE'S BUTTS IN THE RING.
I'LL MAKE YOU A DEAL... I'LL GIVE YOU A PRIVATE LESSON. **JUST** YOU AND ME...
...**IF** YOU HELP WITH THE DISHES TONIGHT.
YEAH, I CAN DO THAT.

DID YOU ALWAYS WANT TO BE A FIGHTER? LIKE, WHEN YOU WERE MY AGE?
YOU CAN'T LAUGH...
...I WANTED TO HAVE A NATURE SHOW... LIKE STEVE IRWIN, BUT MAYBE LESS REPTILES.
EDUCATE PEOPLE ABOUT WHY ANIMALS ARE SO GREAT.
WHAT ABOUT YOU?
ROCKSTAR? HOLLYWOOD ACTRESS?
I DON'T KNOW...
COME ON...
I KIND OF... I KIND OF THINK IT'D BE COOL TO BE A PILOT.
THAT SOUNDS STUPID. LIKE SOMETHING A TODDLER WOULD SAY.
NO WAY. NOT STUPID AT ALL.
I'M TERRIFIED OF FLYING, SO I RESPECT ANYONE WILLINGLY OPERATING ONE OF THOSE THINGS.
WHEN I WAS A KID, I HAD THIS FRIEND IN SCHOOL WHOSE DAD FLEW PLANES.
HE WAS ALWAYS TRAVELING. IN DIFFERENT STATES AND EVEN COUNTRIES.
SOMETIMES SHE GOT TO GO, TOO.
I JUST THOUGHT... IF I WAS A PILOT I COULD GO ANYWHERE I WANT.
BEING A PILOT IS A GOOD GOAL.
YOU THINK WE COULD TRY THOSE DRILLS AGAIN...?

"...I PROMISE I WON'T RUN AWAY THIS TIME."

ELLIE SHOULD BE HERE ANY MINUTE. DID YOU GET YOUR BACKPACK TOGETHER?
IT'S IN THE HALLWAY.
I MADE SURE ALL YOUR CLOTHES ARE PACKED. YOUR GLOVES AND SHIN GUARDS ARE IN THE GYM BAG BY THE DOOR...
I KNOW I'M FORGETTING SOMETHING.
IF WE DID FORGET ANYTHING... YOU'LL BE TEN MINUTES AWAY.
HOW'RE YOU FEELING?
WHAT IF... WHAT IF THEY DON'T LIKE ME?
THAT'S IMPOSSIBLE.
HOW COULD ANYONE NOT LIKE YOU?

I THINK SHE'S HERE. YOU GOT EVERYTHING?
YEAH... I THINK SO.
THANK YOU FOR... EVERYTHING.
IT'S BEEN OUR PLEASURE, MARI. AND WE'LL STILL SEE YOU AT THE GYM EVERY WEEK.
AND YOU CAN CALL LITERALLY ANY TIME.
EVERY DAY IF YOU WANT... MULTIPLE TIMES.
HEY, ELLIE. WE'RE JUST GETTING ALL PACKED UP.
HEY...
...COULD I ACTUALLY TALK WITH THE TWO OF YOU ALONE FOR A MOMENT?

I REALLY DIDN'T WANT TO HAVE TO ASK THIS...
WHAT HAPPENED? I THOUGHT THERE WAS A HOME LINED UP FOR HER.
THERE WAS A... **COMPLICATION.**
FOSTER PARENTS ARE DISQUALIFIED IF THEY HAVE A CRIMINAL HISTORY. WE WERE WORKING FAST TO PLACE MARI IN A HOME...
THEY LIED ON THEIR APPLICATION, BUT FAILED THE BACKGROUND CHECK.
SO, WHAT DOES THIS MEAN? CAN YOU FIND HER ANOTHER HOME?
YES, **EVENTUALLY.** BUT IT WON'T BE TONIGHT.
I NEED TO ASK IF SHE COULD STAY A **LITTLE** LONGER... JUST UNTIL WE GET A NEW SITUATION SORTED FOR HER.
THIS WAS **SUPPOSED** TO BE TEMPORARY.

I THINK--OOF, COME ON, VICTORIA, JUST HOLD STILL FOR TWO MINUTES, PLEASE...
CLARK'S RIGHT. DO YOU HAVE ANY KIND OF TIMELINE FOR WHEN SHE MIGHT BE PLACED IN A NEW HOME?
WE WANT TO HELP, BUT IT'S DEFINITELY TOUGH WITH US BOTH WORKING AND TAKING CARE OF VICTORIA.
WE LOVE HER, ELLIE. SHE IS A GOOD KID IN A BAD SITUATION THAT IS NOT HER FAULT...
WE COULD DEFINITELY TRY TO--
OW!
THIS KID ON THE OTHER HAND...
...SHE CAN BE PRETTY... DIFFICULT.
I THINK I'D TAKE TEN ROUNDS IN THE RING IF IT MEANT I DIDN'T HAVE TO--
KRASH

WHAT WAS THAT?
MARI, ARE YOU--?
MARI?
I THINK WE HAVE A PROBLEM...
...SHE MUST HAVE HEARD EVERYTHING WE SAID.
BUT, I WASN'T EVEN TALKING ABOUT HER, I WAS TALKING ABOUT OUR OWN CHILD BEING DIFFICULT.
WE DON'T KNOW HOW MUCH SHE HEARD OR WHAT SHE THOUGHT...
...AND WE WEREN'T EXACTLY JUMPING TO LET HER STAY.

MARI!
MARI!

CHAPTER 3

SHIT... COME ON... OPEN...
STOP HER!
YOU LITTLE--
HUH?!

GET OFF!
GIVE ME THAT--
UNGH!
YOU SHIT!
KRAK
GAH!

MY NOSE!
47-50 Streets
D F M
SHIT.

A PICKPOCKET WITH A MEAN CROSS...
RELAX, KILLER.
INQUIRING MINDS JUST WANT TO KNOW WHAT YOU'RE DOING OUT SO LATE?
GET AWAY FROM ME...
YOU HUNGRY?
MY FRIEND OWNS A PIZZA PLACE NOT FAR FROM HERE.
PIZZA'S ON ME, BUT YOU'RE LEAVING THE TIP. THAT GUY YOU STOLE FROM CAN AFFORD IT.
"WE CAN'T AFFORD TO WASTE MORE TIME..."

...THEY SAY THE FIRST FORTY-EIGHT HOURS ARE THE MOST CRITICAL IN CASES LIKE THIS...
MISSING
BABE... THAT STATISTIC IS ABOUT CHILDREN WHO ARE TAKEN...
MARI LEFT ON HER OWN AND YOU HEARD WHAT ELLIE SAID ABOUT HER RUNNING OFF A LOT...
HELL, THIS ISN'T EVEN THE FIRST TIME SHE'S RUN OFF ON YOU.
THAT DOESN'T MEAN WE SHOULDN'T CARE...
...CIRCLE THE BLOCK AGAIN.
IKO29T

JO... WE'VE CIRCLED IT FIVE TIMES. SHE'S NOT HERE.
THEN LET'S GO BACK TO THE POLICE STATION.
THEY ASKED US TO LET THEM **WORK.** THEY'RE LOOKING FOR HER BUT YOU SHOWING UP EVERY HOUR ISN'T HELPING.
THEY **AREN'T** LOOKING FOR HER. HE SAID THEY'LL **KEEP AN EYE OUT.**
WHY AM I THE ONLY PERSON WHO CARES ABOUT A MISSING KID?
WE ARE DOING **EVERYTHING** WE CAN. BUT I THINK YOU KNOW BETTER THAN MOST THAT IF MARI DOESN'T **WANT** TO BE FOUND RIGHT NOW...
...THERE'S NOT A WHOLE LOT MORE **WE** CAN DO ABOUT THAT, IS THERE?
CIRCLE THE BLOCK AGAIN.
AS YOU WISH.

YOU READY TO TELL ME WHAT YOU'RE DOING IN THE CITY THIS LATE AT NIGHT...
...OTHER THAN CONNING AN OLD MAN INTO BUYING YOU PIZZA.
I DON'T KNOW. DIDN'T REALLY HAVE ANYWHERE *TO* GO, I GUESS.
WELL, WE CAN AT LEAST CHANGE THAT FOR THE TIME BEING.
FOLLOW ME.
I... I DON'T...

I GET IT. I'M A STRANGE MAN AND IT'S THE MIDDLE OF THE NIGHT.
BUT LET ME LEVEL WITH YOU A LITTLE... OUT OF ALL THE PEOPLE YOU COULD RUN INTO LATE AT NIGHT IN THIS CITY...
...I'D SAY YOU LUCKED OUT MEETING ME.
I SUPPOSE I SHOULD MAKE A MORE FORMAL INTRODUCTION THOUGH.
NAME'S GEORGE PINE. I RUN PINE'S GYM.
WE'RE ALWAYS LOOKING FOR NEW TALENT.
YOUNG PEOPLE WITH A SPARK FOR COMPETITION...
THAT PUNCH YOU THREW BACK IN THE SUBWAY WAS NO ACCIDENT, WAS IT?
YOU'VE GOT SOME KIND OF TRAINING... RAW AND ROUGH... BUT TRAINING NONETHELESS.
SO... KID... I'VE GOT AN OFFER FOR YOU...
YOU CAN COME WITH ME... CHECK OUT THE GYM... HEAR MY PITCH...
OR, YOU CAN GO BACK TO STEALING WALLETS FROM DRUNK IDIOTS ON THE SUBWAY...

"...THE CHOICE IS YOURS."
UNGH!
WHAT'D WE SAY... HUH? CUT TO THE ANGLES.
YOUR TECHNIQUE DOESN'T MEAN SHIT IF YOU'RE NOT HITTIN' THE OTHER GUY, KID!

HRAH!
DON'T STOP!
BREAK DOWN HIS DEFENSE!
THAT'S IT!

STOP...
WHAT THE HELL'RE YOU DOING?
WHAT?
WHY DID YOU STOP?
I WON.
YOU DIDN'T WIN, YOU STOPPED.
THERE'S A DIFFERENCE.
WINNING MEANS LEAVING NO DOUBT.
IT MEANS MAKING SURE THEY CAN NEVER COME AT YOU AGAIN.
BUT... I DON'T WANT TO HURT HIM.

...BUT THERE'S NO ROOM FOR THAT SHIT HERE.
YOUR NAIVETE IS ENDEARING, MARI...
YOU FIGHT FOR ME... YOU WIN FOR ME.
THIS ISN'T A GAME... NOT LIKE YOUR MUAY THAI.
MUAY THAI IS ABOUT CONTROL... RESTRAINT. NONE OF THAT'S REAL.
IN MY RING... IN THE REAL WORLD... YOU WIN BY ANY MEANS NECESSARY, OR YOU'RE OUT.
KOFF
YOU PUNCH UNTIL YOU'RE SURE THE OTHER GUY WILL NEVER PUNCH AGAIN...

"...AND THEN YOU PUNCH ONCE MORE...
"...JUST FOR GOOD MEASURE.
WHAK
"...THAT BAD ATTITUDE OF YOURS...
"...USE IT.
"FUCK CONTROL.
"FUCK RESPECT.

"BECAUSE IN THE REAL WORLD... THEY WOULDN'T STOP PUNCHING YOU IF IT WAS REVERSED.
"SO, ALL THAT ANGER...
"MAKE THEM REGRET STEPPING INTO THAT RING WITH YOU.
THE TRAINING WHEELS ARE OFF.
"NO MORE KID GLOVES.
"THIS IS ABOUT POWER...
"...NOTHING BUT POWER."
"YOU SAW MARI...?"

...YOU SURE IT WAS HER?
SOMEONE FOUND MARI?
YEAH, MAN. AN ADDRESS WOULD BE GREAT.
WHERE IS SHE?
NO, NO... I KNOW WHERE THAT IS.
WHAT THE HELL IS SHE DOING THERE?
WHERE?
WE'LL DEFINITELY CHECK THAT OUT. I APPRECIATE YOU CALLING, ROGER.
I'LL START THE CAR. YOU HAVE AN ADDRESS?
HANG ON A MOMENT, JO. WE NEED TO TALK ABOUT THIS.

TALK ABOUT WHAT? IF YOU KNOW WHERE SHE IS, WE SHOULD--
THAT WAS ROGER.
YOUR OLD ROOMMATE. HE FOUND MARI?
YOU KNOW HOW ROGER HAD THAT...LITTLE PROBLEM WITH GAMBLING FOR A WHILE?
WELL, I GUESS HE'S BACK OFF THAT WAGON... HE WAS AT AN UNDERGROUND MATCH IN THE CITY AND HE SAW A KID WHO KIND OF MATCHES THAT POST YOU MADE ONLINE.
OKAY, GREAT. LET'S GO.
SHE WAS FIGHTING, JO. FOR GEORGE PINE.
I KNOW THAT NAME... WHY DO I KNOW THAT NAME?
GEORGE PINE, BABE. THE BOXER.
2014 HE WAS BANNED FROM ALL I.G.K SANCTIONED EVENTS AFTER HIM AND SOME OF HIS FIGHTERS...
THEY GOT INTO THAT FIGHT IN THE PARKING LOT AFTER LOSING THE TITLE.
THEY PUT A KID IN THE HOSPITAL...

NO WAY... MARI WOULD ***NEVER*** FIGHT FOR A GUY LIKE THAT.
WHY NOT?
THERE'S SOMETHING ELSE YOU NEED TO SEE. LOOKS LIKE PINE'S HOSTING A TOURNAMENT.
HE CAN'T... HE'S ***BANNED*** FROM SANCTIONS IN--
THIS IS DEFINITELY ***NOT*** SANCTIONED.
SMOKERS
Pine's Gym
A ***SMOKER?*** WHAT IS THIS... THE ***EIGHTIES?*** JESUS...
KILL A LOT OF BIRDS WITH JUST ONE STONE...
KEEP HIS FIGHTERS ACTIVE... ACCEPT BETS UNDER THE TABLE...
KEEPING A GYM OPEN IN THE CITY ***CAN'T*** BE CHEAP.
WE ***CAN'T*** LET MARI GET MIXED UP IN THIS...
WE HAVE TO GO GET HER, CLARK...

"...BEFORE SHE GETS HURT."
TEN SECONDS...
OOF!
THWAK
DING DING
LET'S GO... NEXT ROUND STARTS IN THIRTY.
I'M TOO TIRED.
THERE IS NO TIRED ANYMORE. YOU FIGHT THROUGH THAT.
WHEN YOU GO THREE ROUNDS ON SATURDAY, IT WILL FEEL LIKE NOTHING COMPARED TO THIS.
DON'T TELL ME YOU'RE TIRED OF WINNING, CHAMP?

I'M JUST NORMAL TIRED. I'VE BEEN FIGHTING A LOT, MR. PINE.
SLEEP AFTER YOU WIN THE CASH PRIZE, YEAH?
THIS ONE'S THE BIG ONE... WHAT WE'VE BEEN WORKIN' TOWARDS.
YOU CAN DO THIS. YOU HAVEN'T LOST ONE YET, AND WE'RE NOT GONNA START NOW.
OKAY. HOW MANY MORE ROUNDS?
AS MANY AS IT TAKES.
AS MANY AS IT TAKES.
WHO'S THE BEST?
I AM.
DING DING
I'M THE BEST.

ATTA GIRL!
JAB!
FOLLOW WITH THAT CROSS!
MARI!
MARI, STOP!
OOF!

HEY! WHO THE HELL ARE YOU?!
MARI... ARE YOU OKAY?
GET AWAY FROM MY FIGHTER!
WHAT ARE YOU DOING HERE?
I CAME TO TAKE YOU HOME SO WE COULD--
HOME? I DON'T HAVE A HOME.
WHAT YOU SAID MADE THAT VERY CLEAR.
NO... MARI, WHAT YOU HEARD... I WASN'T TALKING ABOUT YOU.
I'M SORRY THAT YOU EVER THOUGHT I WOULDN'T WANT YOU AROUND.
I DON'T NEED YOU. JUST LEAVE.

I'M NOT ASKING... YOU HAVE TO LEAVE.
YOU CAN'T STAY HERE.
YOU ARE NOT MY MOM!
I'M TRYING TO HELP YOU. IF YOU STAY HERE, YOU'LL GET HURT.
THIS ISN'T THE RIGHT WAY TO FIGHT.
YOU'RE NOT READY, MARI.
I'VE ALREADY PROVEN THAT I AM READY. I HAVEN'T LOST A SINGLE FIGHT YET.
IF YOU DON'T COME WITH ME, I WILL CALL ELLIE AND--
HAVE ME SENT AWAY?
NO... I WOULDN'T...
GET OUT OF MY GYM AND STOP HARASSING MY FIGHTER.
YOU HEARD THE GIRL...

"...SHE WANTS TO FIGHT."
WE'VE GOT A PACKED HOUSE OUT THERE!
YOU READY TO DO THIS THING?
I'M READY.

NEXT UP...
...THE ONLY ALL-FEMALE BOUT OF THE EVENING!
WE CAN'T LET HER DO THIS... THIS IS INSANE.
I KNOW, J... BUT YOU ALREADY TRIED STOPPING HER ONCE AND HOW'D THAT GO?

MARI WANTS TO DO THE EXACT OPPOSITE OF WHAT YOU WANT...
NOT GOOD.
THAT MAKES NO SENSE. I'M TRYING TO HELP HER...
OH, THAT MAKES NO SENSE TO YOU? HAVE YOU EVER MET A TEENAGER BEFORE?
AND NOW HER OPPONENT FOR THE EVENING...
...FORMER STRAWWEIGHT CHAMPION OF THE WORLD...
...JESSICA ANDRE!

YOU'VE GOT TO BE FUCKING KIDDING ME...
LET'S GO!
IT'S HER. THAT'S...

...ANNNND YOUR NEW CHAMPION...
JESSICA ANDRE!
HEY... HEY, YOU DID GOOD.
YOU DID YOUR ABSOLUTE BEST.
DON'T BULLSHIT ME.
YOU PLAYED HER GAME. YOU LET HER DICTATE THE RULES... AND YOU LOST CONTROL, J.
BUT THAT DOESN'T MEAN YOU'RE A BAD FIGHTER...
I LOST.

I LOST.
ALL RIGHT... WE'RE GOING TO HAVE A GOOD, CLEAN FIGHT...
SURE. GOOD AND CLEAN.
WE HAVE TO STOP THIS.

THE FIGHTERS STUDY ONE ANOTHER... LOOKING FOR OPENINGS...
...AND ANDRE STRIKES FIRST WITH A JAB!
ANDRE TESTING THE WATERS...
ANDRE HAS THE KID ON THE ROPES!
BUT SHE'S NOT OUT YET...
...THE KID STRIKES BACK HARD!

DING
...AND ANDRE DIVES RIGHT IN!
ANDRE IS JUST **PEPPERING** HER OPPONENT... SHE CLEARLY SMELLS BLOOD!
USING THE ROPES FOR LEVERAGE...
ANDRE CLEARLY UNPREPARED FOR THAT HIT!
AND NOW ANDRE IS ON THE DEFENSIVE! SHE UNDERESTIMATED THE NEWCOMER!

I CAN'T WATCH...
MAYBE YOU SHOULD... BECAUSE MARI'S ACTUALLY HOLDING HER OWN.
OOF!
DING
BACK TO YOUR CORNERS!

SHE DID OKAY IN THERE.
JESSICA IS GOING TO TRY TO **MURDER** HER IN THE NEXT ROUND.
I HAVE TO STOP THE FIGHT.
GEORGE IS GOING TO BE PISSED...
...HE BET **EVERYTHING** ON ANDRE AND THAT KID MADE HER LOOK LIKE AN AMATEUR.
DIDN'T HE SAY SHE DIDN'T HAVE A CHANCE IN HELL...
WELL, THE KID'S BEEN DOIN' OKAY IN THOSE OTHER BOUTS.
SERIOUSLY? YOU THINK ANY OF THAT WAS **REAL?**
GEORGE'S BEEN **PAYING** PEOPLE TO TAKE A DIVE. MAKE THE KID LOOK GOOD... THEN BET AGAINST HER WHEN HE KNOWS SHE WON'T WIN.
NO...
NO!

WHAT'RE YOU DOING IN THERE?!
WHAT? I'M WINNING.
YOU'RE SWINGING AROUND LIKE A GODDAMN GOON!
IS THAT WHAT YOU WANT PEOPLE TO THINK YOU ARE? YOU WANT PEOPLE TO--?
MARI!
HEY, GET OUTTA HERE... WE ALREADY TOLD YOU--
THE FIGHT'S RIGGED AGAINST YOU!
WHAT ARE YOU DOING HERE?
GET AWAY FROM MY RING, HUH?
THEY ARE BETTING AGAINST YOU. YOU'RE SUPPOSED TO LOSE THE FIGHT.
YOU'RE HERE TO LOSE.
I'VE NEVER LOST.
ADMIT IT, GEORGE... ADMIT THAT NONE OF THOSE OTHER FIGHTS WERE REAL.
MARI ONLY WON BECAUSE YOU PAID PEOPLE TO LOSE.
IS... IS THAT TRUE? I THOUGHT...
DON'T TAKE IT PERSONALLY, MARI. WE MAKE MORE MONEY THIS WAY... IT'S GOOD FOR BOTH OF US.

NONE OF THOSE FIGHTS... THEY WEREN'T REAL.
NO...
I DIDN'T COME HERE TO LOSE.
MARI, JUST THINK ABOUT THIS AND--
SHUT UP.
FIGHTERS TO THE CENTER...
NO... MARI, YOU CAN'T GO BACK IN THERE.
MARI, WAIT...
...IF YOU'RE GOING TO DO IT... DO IT RIGHT.
I KNOW ANDRE. SHE'S A BRAWLER. YOU CAN'T BEAT THAT WITH POWER...
...YOU HAVE TO BE CONTROLLED.
LET HER BE WILD... AND USE THAT AGAINST HER.
DING

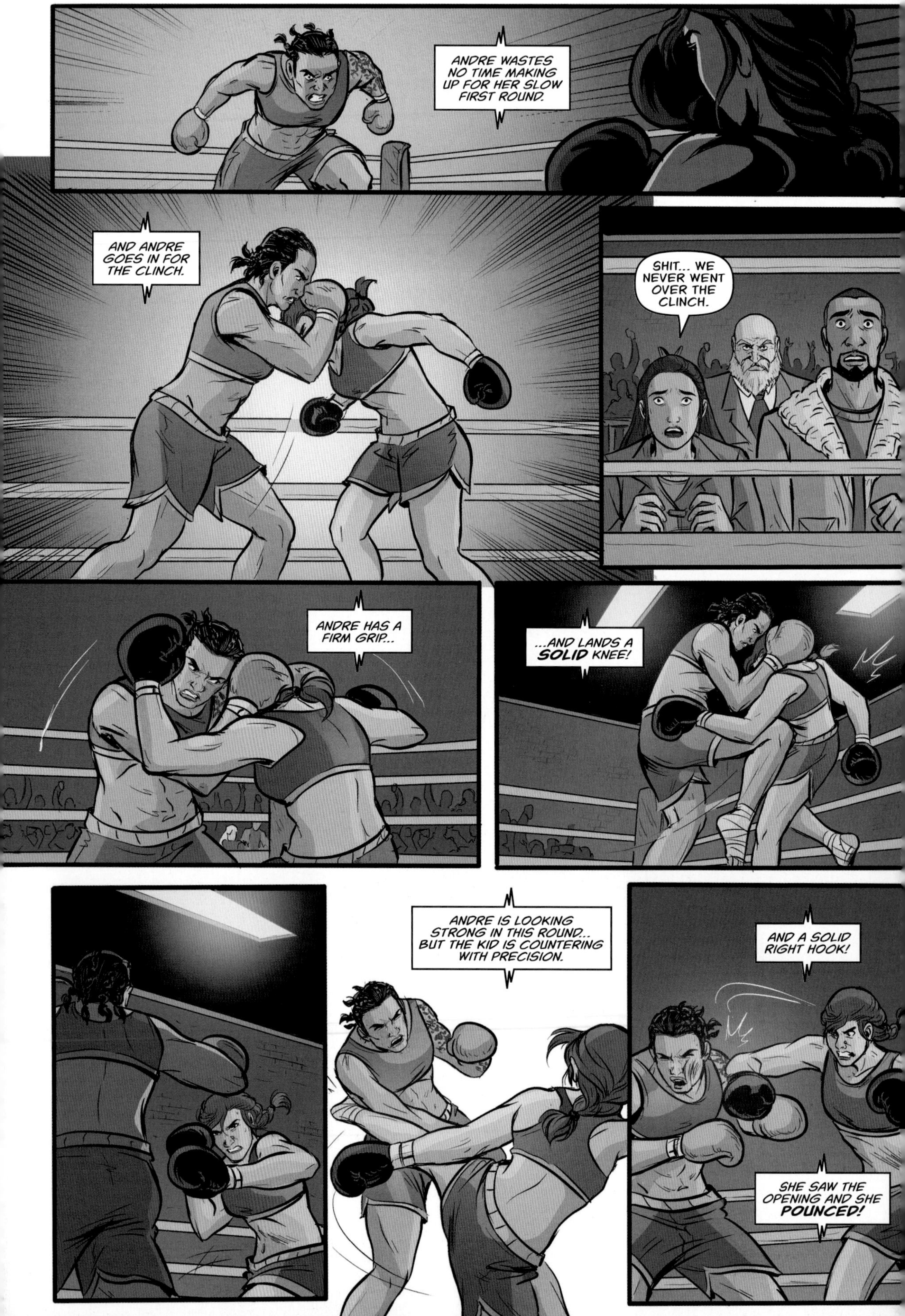
ANDRE WASTES NO TIME MAKING UP FOR HER SLOW FIRST ROUND.
AND ANDRE GOES IN FOR THE CLINCH.
SHIT... WE NEVER WENT OVER THE CLINCH.
ANDRE HAS A FIRM GRIP...
...AND LANDS A SOLID KNEE!
ANDRE IS LOOKING STRONG IN THIS ROUND... BUT THE KID IS COUNTERING WITH PRECISION.
AND A SOLID RIGHT HOOK!
SHE SAW THE OPENING AND SHE POUNCED!

AND THERE'S ANDRE... TRYING THE CLINCH AGAIN!
SETTING UP FOR ANOTHER KNEE...
KRAK

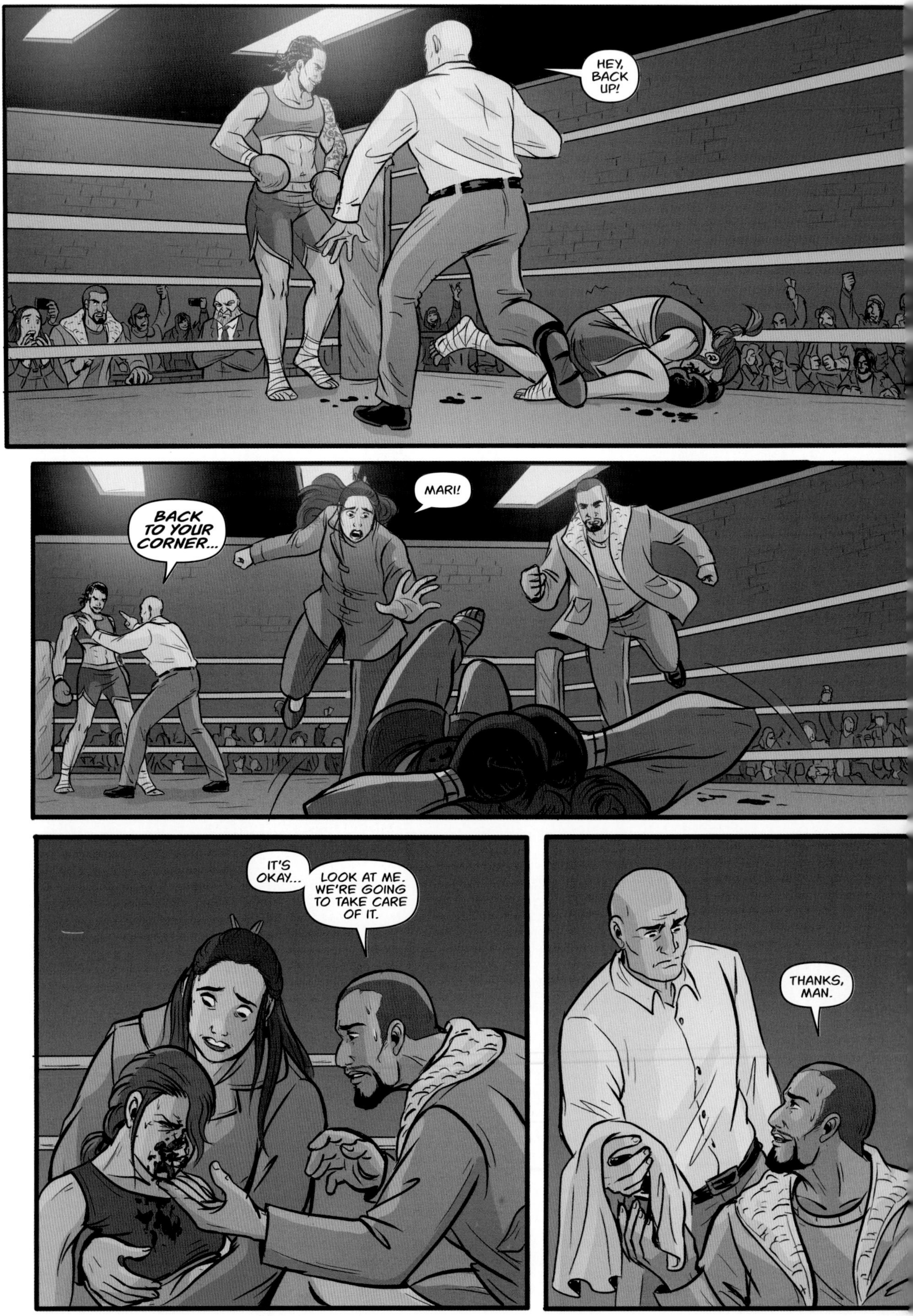
HEY, BACK UP!
BACK TO YOUR CORNER...
MARI!
IT'S OKAY...
LOOK AT ME. WE'RE GOING TO TAKE CARE OF IT.
THANKS, MAN.

THAT'S IT... WE JUST NEED TO KEEP SOME PRESSURE ON THERE--
JOANNA CARR?
DIDN'T I TAKE YOUR BELT?
NOW YOU WANT ME TO BEAT UP YOUR KID, TOO?
DON'T.
SHE THREW AN ILLEGAL HIT.
DOESN'T MATTER NOW... WE'RE DONE HERE.
I GUESS LOSING TO ME IS SOME KIND OF FAMILY TRADITION.
IF I HAD KNOWN SHE WAS YOURS, I WOULD HAVE DONE MORE THAN BREAK HER NOSE.
YOU'RE A CHEATER. NOTHING MORE.

THEN FIGHT ME.
DON'T DO IT, JO...
ONE ROUND. PROVE THAT YOU NEVER DESERVED THAT BELT IN THE FIRST PLACE.
YOU HAVE NOTHING TO PROVE, JOANNA.
I NEED GLOVES.

THIS IS A BAD IDEA.
SHE TOOK MY TITLE. THE LAST FIGHT OF MY CAREER...
AND SHE HURT MARI.
I'M NOT LETTING HER WIN. NOT AGAIN.
YOU KNOW THAT DOESN'T MATTER, BABE. WHAT HAPPENS IN THE RING... THAT'S NOT WHAT DETERMINES WHO ACTUALLY WINS.
CLARK...
I KNOW... YOU WANT TO DO THIS.
YOU HAVE MORE IN COMMON WITH MARI THAN YOU THINK.
THIS WILL BE A CLEAN FIGHT. ONE ILLEGAL THROW FROM EITHER OF YOU...
...AND YOU'RE OUT.
DO YOU UNDERSTAND?
YEAH.

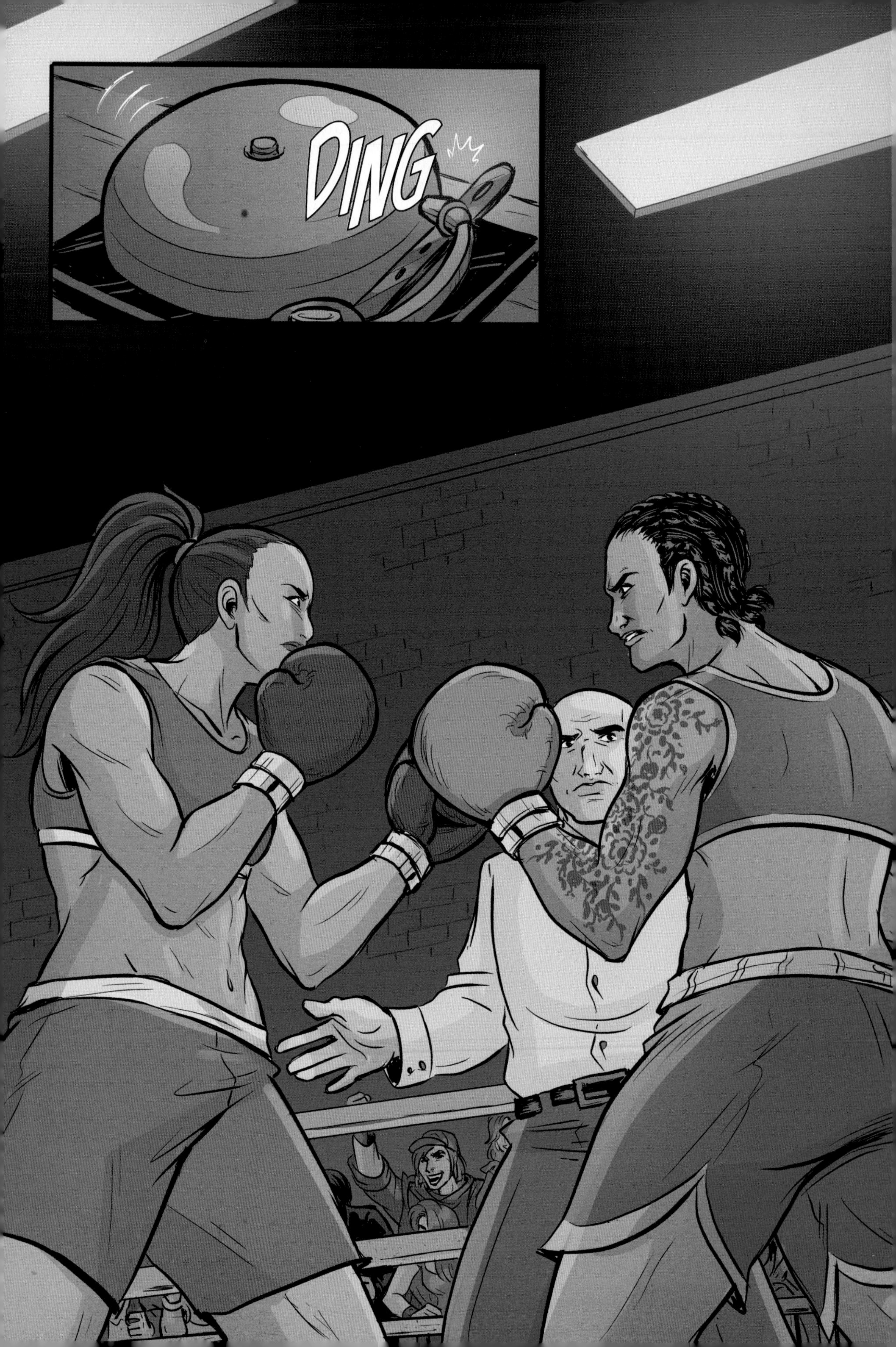
DING

ANDRE STRIKES FIRST...
...FORCING CARR IMMEDIATELY ON THE DEFENSIVE.
BUT CARR CAPITALIZES ON ANDRE'S OWN MOMENTUM...
THAT'S IT, JO! JUST BE PATIENT!
...MOMENTARILY SHAKING ANDRE'S FLURRY.
ANDRE TRYING TO GET BACK TO HER STRONG OFFENSIVE POSITIONING.
AND ANDRE LANDS A LIVER SHOT!

BUT CARR WASTES NO TIME RESPONDING...
...DODGING A LEFT KICK FROM ANDRE.
CARR CATCHES ANDRE OFF BALANCE WITH A STRONG TEEP TO THE CHEST...
...BREAKING HER DEFENSE DOWN WITH PATIENCE THAT ANDRE CLEARLY WASN'T EXPECTING FROM HER OPPONENT.
ANDRE'S PLAN SEEMS TO BE TO BULLY HER OPPONENT...
...BUT CARR ISN'T THROWN OFF BY IT IN THE SLIGHTEST.

AND ANDRE GOES DOWN!
DING
WHAK
NO!
HRAH!
HEY! WHAT DID I TELL YOU?!

IF SHE LEAVES THE RING, SHE'S DISQUALIFIED!
SHE'S ACTUALLY RIGHT. YOU HAVE TO STAY HERE UNTIL THE JUDGES ARE DONE DELIBERATING, OR I HAVE TO DISQUALIFY YOU.

I WIN!
YOU ALL SAW IT! SHE LEFT!
YOU KNOW YOU WON THAT ROUND, RIGHT? YOU COULD HAVE BEATEN HER YEARS AGO, TOO.
MAYBE. BUT MAYBE NOT...
YOUR WINNER... JESSICA ANDRE!
...IT DOESN'T REALLY MATTER.
OH GOD... YOU'RE GOING TO SAY SOMETHING TOTALLY CHEESY ABOUT HOW WINNING DOESN'T ACTUALLY MATTER... BLAH BLAH BLAH.
OH NO, WINNING IS GREAT. BUT I WON WITH OR WITHOUT THE BELT...

"...I WON BY FINDING MY *FAMILY.*"
I COULDN'T FIND MY RED WRAPS. HAVE YOU SEEN--?
LAUNDRY ROOM. WHERE YOU LEFT THEM.
OH, THAT'S RIGHT.
AND... YOU WON'T TELL ELLIE ABOUT...?
ABOUT YOU FIGHTING IN AN UNSANCTIONED, UNDERGROUND BETTING TOURNAMENT IN NEW YORK CITY?
NO, WE WON'T SAY ANYTHING.
I'M NOT EXACTLY SURE I WAS THE PARADIGM OF GOOD PARENTAL RESPONSIBILITY ANYWAYS.
WHAT TIME IS ELLIE PICKING ME UP TOMORROW?
ABOUT THAT...

WE TOLD ELLIE NOT TO COME.
WHAT...? WHY?
WE GOT YOU A WELCOME PRESENT.
BUT... ISN'T THIS...?
JUST OPEN IT.
KSSSH
REPORT OF ADOPTION
STATE OF NEW JERSEY
I DON'T UNDERSTAND...
...YOU'RE... ADOPTING ME?

WELCOME HOME, MARI.
THE END.